MY TEACHER IS A WEREWOLF

For Ollie and Jude

*Who are quite possibly two
of the bravest boys I have ever known.*

Without you, this would merely be a story.

*Instead it's a heart-warming experience of
magic, courage and real life!*

So thank you for always allowing me to listen.

To all children, everywhere

Who have ever felt scared, sad or shy.

Who have felt even the tiniest wave of anxiety.

*Never underestimate the power of being five, or eight, or even
fifteen, because you have the ability to change teachers into
werewolves and headmasters into vampires.*

And that is not only very clever, but truly magic!

(Just don't forget to turn them back again).

Copyright 2020 by Hayley Jones
Published by Poppy Publishing
ISBN: 978-1-9163188-9-2

Illustrations by Mary Dark

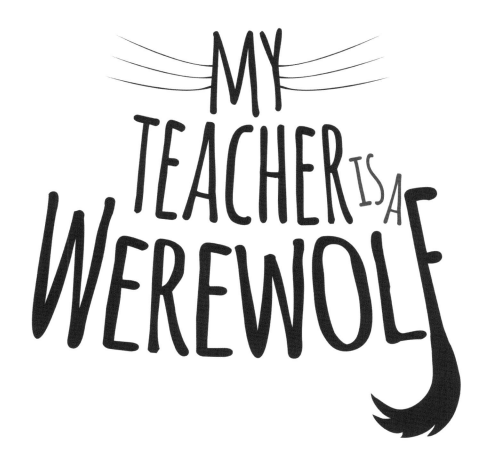

MY TEACHER IS A WEREWOLF

ILLUSTRATED BY

MARY DARK

WRITTEN BY

HAYLEY JONES

PUBLISHED BY

Poppy Publishing

I'm starting school in September, it's time that I embark,
The gates are painted pencils and the playground's like a park.
I hear that there's a library, I hear the lunch is great,
I get to have school dinners and sit with my best mate.

On Tuesday it's a forest walk and Wednesday it is show and talk. On Thursdays we get laptops out, Fridays we get to play about. Numeracy and Literacy are each and every day, I can't wait to learn this part, to reach my dreamy job one day!

There's only one small problem,
well actually it's rather scary,
I saw my teacher on induction
day and she was rather hairy.

It sprouted from her ears, which were
pointy on her head, her teeth were sharp
and sparkly, the type you really dread!

Her eyes were amber, brown and gold, her nose
looked black and wet,
All of her skin thick with FUR, she looked like
my neighbours pet!

I'm afraid to share this news next,
but I really can't resist,
Miss Juniper's not your usual type,

Miss Juniper...

...looks...

like...

How can I go to class with her? I've told my Mum you see. But she just giggles like I'm telling jokes and gently snuggles me.

I told my best mate Tim, but he was desperate for a wee.

I elbowed Florence so she'd look up, but she poked out her tongue at me!

If nobody will listen, I'll simply have to brave it.
Tomorrow it's a stay and play and I intend to survive it!

I've decided not to bath tonight, I don't want to smell
too yummy. Maybe I'll skip breakfast too I don't want
my clothes all crumby.

Morning comes and I start to worry, that funny tummy feel.

Mum brings me in some cheese on toast but I decline the meal.

I get dressed in my dullest clothes I do NOT want to stand out.

I promise myself to sit really still and not to muck about.

It's time to leave, I walk with Tim, he's dressed so very smart,

The mummies chat behind us, they say we melt their hearts.

15

We approach the gate our door is first the children are going in, and there she is Miss Juniper with her toothy grin!

My body feels so very small, my
confidence is low,
School isn't feeling quite the same,
I should have just said no.

I hold mum's hand, I take a breath and there Miss Juniper stands.

She says: "Good morning Henry, welcome back,
please go and find some toys, I will be in soon to
fetch a snack for all you girls and boys."

Her voice was not what I remembered, it sounded rather sweet.
Her smile was much less toothy now and this time
she wore shoes on her feet.

Mum eases me through the door,
she looks all super proud,

I see my friends all playing games,
there was really quite a crowd.

20

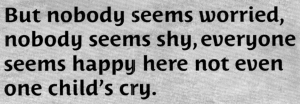

But nobody seems worried, nobody seems shy, everyone seems happy here not even one child's cry.

Was it just me who felt like this? I just don't understand, Miss Juniper is a werewolf, from school she should be banned!

"Snack time," I hear Miss Juniper call and some children sit on the mat,
I choose to stick with mum, she's always got my back.

She begins to hand out oranges and a tiny little drink, she's making a beeline to give me some, my body can't help but shrink!

Mum says: "Henry please take your snack" - clearly doesn't have my back.

I open my hands carefully and keep my eyes shut tight.
I expect to feel a hairy touch, I hope she doesn't bite.
But no, they feel all normal, hands that are regular and plain,
ten fingers and pretty finger nails, I really can't complain.
I open my eyes and thank her, she smiles, so I'll sit down.
Maybe she's not so bad - even if she's furry and brown.

I sit with my friends and chat a bit, snack time is nearly done,
The best part about it all, is I think I'm having fun.

After snack there's so many toys, and our mums go and socialise.
I play away with little fear, which comes as a real surprise.

There's so many things
to learn about, like where
to find our hooks, how to
work the laptops out and
safely store our books.

We meet our classroom
helper, we explore all
of the toys,

I absolutely love it and
I've met some nice new
girls and boys.

Stay and Play is almost done, we sit down for circle time.
We read a story about three bears and sing a little rhyme.
Suddenly I realise - Miss Juniper has lost her fur, her eyes are
blue and smiley, sharp teeth do not occur!
She looks completely normal and super teacher like,
Her clothes are cute, her hair is neat, there's nothing to dislike.

I got it wrong, I must admit, I really was mistaken,
My fears took over, my heart felt tight, I got myself all shaken.
It's time to leave, I get my things and boldly leave with pride,
My head's held high, I'm smiling big, I no longer want to hide.
My mum is proud, she smiles and waves when I see her from afar,
I leave the class with a new book and we get a sticky star.

We walk on home, I'm all relaxed,
there's no need to be hurried.

Tim says "Miss Juniper is so nice,
but I really am quite worried."

"Why?" I ask all confused, Tim seemed so super ready.
"Didn't you see, the head of the school? We'll have to tread real steady"
I had no idea what Tim was saying, the headteacher seemed so nice.
"To have a vampire rule the school, it's time we took advice."
I decide not to tell Tim and wait, he'll soon realise,
Sometimes when you're scared of things, kindness can disguise.

Sometimes when things are new it makes your body weird.
Your brain goes crazy, you feel all scared and normal things are feared.
But that's ok, there's always time to figure out our problems.
There's always someone to listen close and share some words of wisdom.

So share your feelings, try new things and at school you shall see,
That maybe that scary vampire, isn't what he seems to be.